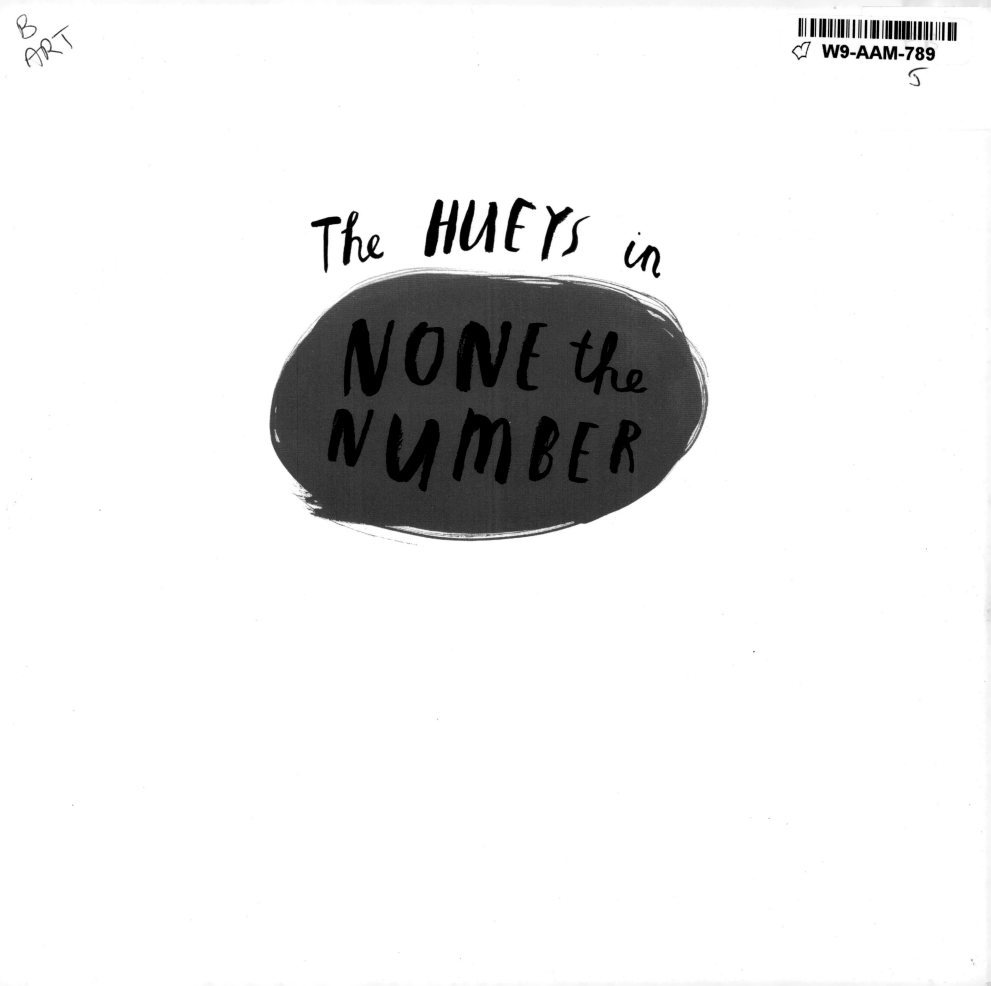

The HUEYS in

NONE the NUMBER

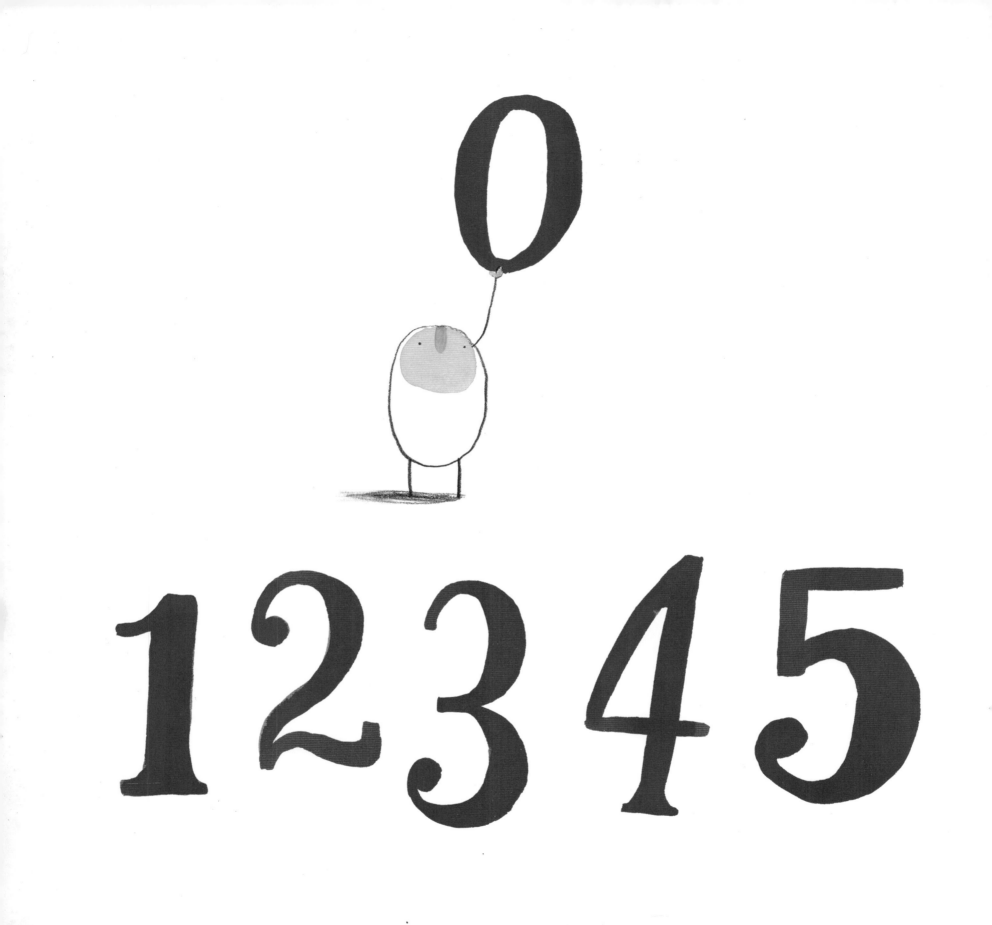

6 7 8 9 10

For Frieda

www.oliverjeffersworld.com

First published in hardback in Great Britain by HarperCollins Children's Books in 2014
First published in paperback in 2014

10 9 8 7 6 5 4 3 2 1

ISBN: 978-0-00-756711-9

HarperCollins Children's Books is a division of HarperCollins Publishers Ltd.

Text and illustrations copyright © Oliver Jeffers 2014

With thanks to James Martin for the additional text on page 31

Visit our website at: www.harpercollins.co.uk

Printed and bound in China

The HUEYS in

NONE the NUMBER

OLIVER JEFFERS

HarperCollins *Children's Books*

"How many lumps of cheese
do you see just there?"

"Um... I don't see any."

"Of course.
It's one less
than one."

"I see.
So one more
than none is...
one?"

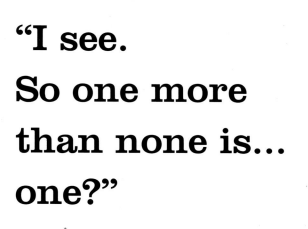

"That's right...

Like that ONE light blue phone over there.

1

If you add another ONE you have TWO,
like two sleeps until the big day.

3

After that,
it's THREE,
like my collection
of chairs.

Then FOUR. That's how many tantrums Kevin throws every day.

FIVE hats that Rupert has to choose from.

 **SIX fishermen
waiting for
the bus.**

**SEVEN oranges I balanced
on some things yesterday.**

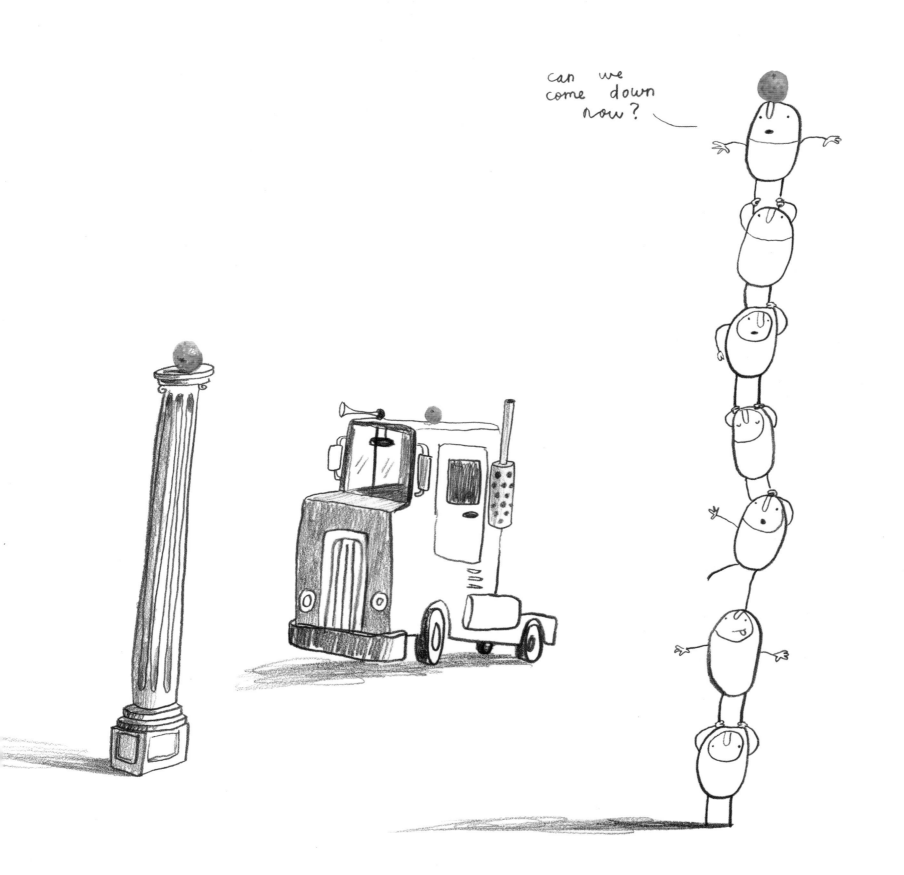

EIGHT party guests trying to guess the gift.

NINE seagulls that are after Frank's chips.

10

TEN trumpeters walking by.

Quite a spectacle,
when you put it
all together."

"Ooh."

"But when you take them all away...

...you get NONE."

"Oh."

"Is none a number?"

012345

6 7 8 9 10

So is 'none' really a number?

To a mathematician, zero might be the most important number there is.

The ancient Egyptians and Babylonians already had symbols corresponding to zero. The oldest known text using 0 as a digit in a decimal system like our own is from 5th century India. Ancient Greek philosophers worried about whether zero was really a number – how can nothing be something? Some even thought that 1 should not qualify, claiming 2 as the smallest number.

Zero is an *integer* (whole number) – the only one which is neither positive nor negative. The *natural numbers* or *counting numbers* are sometimes taken to be {0, 1, 2, 3,…} and sometimes {1, 2, 3, 4,…} – whether to include zero is a matter of taste and convention. As you can see from this book, there's a good argument for including zero in the counting numbers, because 'none' is sometimes the right answer when you're asked to count something.

Also look out for these brilliant picture books!